A Child at Heart

Susan Fitzgerald

A Child at Heart

Acknowledgements

Thanks to Zenda Vecchio, who mentors and facilitates with such grace and style, for providing an enjoyable arena for me to experiment with my writing and for encouraging me to publish this book. She spent some time reading all the stories and making helpful suggestions.

Also to the Nairne U3A Writing Group, past and present, for the support, camaraderie and general hilarity I've enjoyed each week for close on four years.

And to the Tuesday U3A Writing Group, for added input and friendly inclusion.

A Child at Heart
ISBN 978 1 74027 880 5
Copyright © text Susan Fitzgerald 2014
Cover image © adrenalinapura – Fotolia.com

First published 2014
Reprinted 2017

GINNINDERRA PRESS
PO Box 3461 Port Adelaide 5015
www.ginninderrapress.com.au

Contents

Dedicated to the Joy of Writing

Boys Will Be Boys

Arrested

'Have you got the sausages?' Pete whispered.

I nodded, my mouth too dry to talk even though we were on the other side of the fence.

They were for the dog. We were trying to befriend it, as its yapping would bring Old Man McCafferty out onto the veranda, yelling that he'd either shoot us or have us arrested. That was the thrill. To be able to get through the fence, avoid the dog, climb the tree, pick the peaches and escape was both the challenge and the delight we faced this summer. Last year, some boys had done it and are still continually bragging about it, but we haven't noticed them here for a second try any time we've come.

It'd been my idea to make friends with the dog. The only trouble was that, as soon as he either spotted us or smelt us, he started his crazy barking. So we'd kept watch from the old pine tree across the street and waited until Old Maccy, as he was known by all the local kids, went shopping. We were hoping he would take the dog. If he did, we had a clear go at the peaches – unless he came back, that is. He was known to be tricky. He'd leave it, though, we reckoned, to guard the peaches. It was rumoured to bite.

He'd left some minutes ago and we were at the fence trying to see the dog. Pete had found a knothole and pushed it out. No dog.

Pete whistled, he was good at that. He had been practising to sound like Old Maccy. The dog came around the house.

'Must have been seeing off Old Maccy at the front,' I whispered.

Pete nodded and whistled again, then, as the dog started hesitantly towards us, indicated with his arm that I throw over a sausage. It landed clear of the dog, but close enough to get its attention. It trotted over, sniffed it and started to eat. Pete whistled again. It came trotting over then and I lobbed another one. After that one, it came to the fence. I pushed another one under the railing where we'd dug a hole. Finishing that one, it stuck its nose under the fence.

'Hungry dog,' I said and let it smell and lick my fingers.

Then Pete, whistling softly, offered his.

'We should pat it and we'll need to loosen a plank for that,' I said as I reached for the small crowbar I'd borrowed from Dad's shed.

Pete levered it loose at the bottom rail.

'Don't break it,' I cautioned. 'We don't want the dog to get out.'

'Too big,' grunted Pete as he worked on the plank higher up at the next rail.

With a creaking rip, the plank came away from that rail and hung loosely from the top one.

'Good it's an old fence,' said Pete laying down the crowbar and reaching to pat the dog, whistling low again, rubbing in all the dog-loved places.

One more sausage, more patting and we were on the way to having a friend.

'We'll be back tomorrow with more,' Pete said to it and then, turning to me, 'The old man goes to the pub for lunch on Thursdays, got that from Ted.'

I nodded. Pete had it all planned.

He finished with 'We'll be OK for Friday.'

The plan was to come then, just after dinner, when the quiz show came on telly. I'd heard Mum say McCafferty watched it as he'd won something a few years ago. More sausages, more patting, just to be sure. If our plan worked, we'd be back again Saturday when he went to the footy.

Trouble was, we hadn't figured on Old Maccy being so wise to us. We'd come both Thursday and Friday and the whistle and sausages brought the dog again. We'd prised away two more planks so we could get in and out, and carried a big rock to hold them in place so the dog wouldn't break out. My idea again; Pete says my head must be full of them. So everything seemed great.

Now, come Saturday, we are stuck up the tree, with peaches up our jumpers and juice running down our chins.

'Bin feedin' ma bleeding dog, have ya, ya little mongrels?' Old Man McCafferty stood on the veranda with what looked awfully like a shotgun, yelling his block off. He kicked the dog, 'Useless mutt,' then started towards us, waving a definite shotgun above his head. 'I'll fix ya, ya little blighters. Steal ma peaches, will ya? Thought I wasn't ready for ya tricks, eh?'

'What'll we do?' said Pete wildly looking at me and Old Maccy both in turn. 'Find one of your ideas, quick!'

So I used what was most handy, saying, 'That's if he's really going to shoot,' and started to pelt him with the peaches.

Down he went, tripped over the dog trying to avoid my barricade, dropped the gun and it went off.

In terror we slid down the tree and raced for the fence. The dog, in deference to its master, turned against us and ripped my trousers nearly off. We didn't stop to wedge the rock. Blow the dog.

Scraped, shaken and laughing in bravado, we hid in the bushes at the back of my place and ate the two squashed peaches I'd put up my sleeve.

'Well, we didn't get arrested,' Pete garbled around his peach.

'Not this time,' I grinned back. 'I wonder if he fired blanks?'

Quarry

They were after him, the whole pack of them. He could hear their howls as they closed in. He pedalled faster, so glad his dad was rich and had bought him a bike with really good gears. At first, he had sprinted blindly away from them, but now he knew where he was heading. Hopefully, this hill would slow them down.

'We're gonna get you, city boy.' That would be Brett, the leader of the pack. 'Don't think your toffy city bike can get you away from us.'

So, he thought, it was working. They were dropping behind.

They had picked on him from the first day. He'd known it would be difficult, that he'd be seen as different. But it was only on that first day at the new school he'd realised how much. Wrong hair, wrong clothes, wrong shoes and, most of all, wrong bike. He'd been so proud of this bike when he'd finally got it. It was the right kind or better at his old school. There, it had finally given him the approval of that gang, the approval he'd wanted so much. He knew his mum had struggled since his dad left years ago and she really did her best. But the bike he'd desperately wanted had been beyond her, so he'd asked his dad even though he knew it would hurt his mum. When he rode it to school that first day, it had felt so good. But here, the bike was too damn good. Now, though, this same bike was hurtling him up this hill way in front of them. He knew in the pit of his stomach they would still get him eventually, even if he got away today.

Made it! Finally he'd reached the top and the wire fence that enclosed the old quarry. He'd found this place last weekend. Now, where was that broken part of the fence?

'We're on ta ya, mate. Won't be long now,' came the taunt floating up the hill.

Not much time. He skidded into a swing, moving into the other direction and pedalling furiously around to where he remembered the break was. Throwing his bike down, fully knowing it would probably not be the same after they got to it, he scrambled through the gap, ripping his new uniform in the process. He groaned. How his mum would rant.

Steadying himself, and remembering the coaching from the abseiling and climbing classes he'd attended last year when on holiday with Dad, he disappeared over the edge. Hand over hand, feet feeling for any footholds, carefully, but as fast as he could, he started down the cliff face.

Out of earshot, the other bikes slid to a stop in the gravel on the opposite side.

Brett burst out with 'Shit, look at him!' overriding the gasps of the others as they watched their quarry moving confidently down the sheer cliff face.

Looks of admiration grudgingly began blossoming on all their faces.

'Not bad,' Brett said. 'Give him that.'

I Got It Down To a Fine Art

I'm nine. I stand on the lawn in front of our house, arms akimbo. I'm studying the roof line and audaciously plotting my escape route. I need to meet with our new gang at nine o'clock, half an hour after my bedtime. We're going to meet in the old abandoned timber mill down by the river. This is our temporary club house.

It's ten minutes to nine and I creep out of bed and put on my sneakers. I'm already dressed, because I didn't put on my pyjamas and I pulled up the covers before Mum came to say good night. I open the dormer window and gingerly climb out, avoiding looking around…yet. I lower myself down to the small balcony below it and drop the last distance, landing with a soft thump. I cock my head, listening for any indication that the sound had been heard. All seems quiet, so I climb over the balcony rail and start to creep across the sloped tiles up towards the ridge line of the lower level of the house. I'm nearly there and my sneakers lose their grip and my foot slips. I grab frantically and I'm able to reach the ridgepole. I lie panting, my heart hammering, listening again for the half-suspected detection by my mother. Nothing.

'Next time, bare feet,' I intone. 'Better grip, sneakers around my neck,' I pant.

I lie there, quietened now. I look up and take a deep breath. I see all the stars gleaming in the huge night sky and feel a sense of awe and wonder. Heaving myself up, I crouch on the ridge line and slowly move into an upright position.

'I can do this. I can do this,' I chant.

Slowly, placing my feet carefully in line, I make my way along until

I'm near where the large oak tree's branch hangs near the house. Dad's dad planted it in the backyard when the house was built. I lower myself to sitting again and slowly slide down the roof until I can take hold of the branch. It's too thin this close, so I lean out and taking hold of it where it's thicker, swing out and grab it with my legs. I hang there upside down for a moment, feeling like Tarzan in the jungle movies. Then I remember Buddy and Jim making their own way to the club house. I pull myself up and shimmy across the branch until it meets the trunk. I look down at the drop to the ground. Shit, I've forgotten how high it is. Even if I hang down, the drop will still be more than my height. I'm stymied for a minute until I remember the cowboy movie I saw last weekend and how he dropped down from the roof and rolled away as he fell. So I let go, aiming to roll as soon as the ground touches my feet. It's all too sudden and I'm lying on my back winded, gasping for breath and wondering if I have any broken bones. I roll over and stand up, brushing myself off.

Hey! I did it, my thoughts shout to me. I'd better find a rope for next time, though. I race to the back fence and pry apart the loose paling and nip down the back lane as fast as I can.

I'm fifteen and it's been a few years since I did the roof thing but I want to meet up with the guys and go to the party at the beach. That new girl Charlene? Yeah, Charlene, will be there. I open the dormer window and clamber out. I lower myself down and I'm surprised my feet touch the balcony floor. I climb over the balcony rail and, crouching over, reach the ridgepole in three strides, my bare feet gripping the tiles easily. Rising up, I stand balancing on the ridge line, remembering all the times I'd walked across with arms outstretched like a tightrope walker. I swing easily over to the branch and look down from the old tree. I'm pretty sure I don't need the rope swing. I smile as I remember asking for it, not letting on my real reason for the rope. I lower myself down, let go and am again surprised at how short the drop is.

I go out the side gate and forget about Old MacGinty's dog. Bloody hell! I run like mad as his barking reaches into the night. Next time, some sausages or a chop!

I'm eighteen and I've got this roof escapade down to a fine art. I show Charlene how good I am at it.

I'm thirty-five and I open the dormer window and drop down to the balcony and sit in the old chair I've put there. It's good to get away from Charlene and the kids for a bit. All those stars… I drink in the night. All those years of perfecting the art of roof walking… I smile and raise my glass to those boys in distant past.

Terrorists

I didn't know where they would be coming from next. My heart was pounding and I felt breathless with panic. It took all my courage to stay hidden behind the wall and not make a run for it. I tried to calm myself so the pounding of my blood wouldn't be so loud in my ears. I needed to be able to hear them coming.

Why was I here? Why had I put myself in this situation? I had all my dreams and hopes yet I couldn't be sure now that any of them would come true.

Then I heard them. They were coming. Blood-curdling yells that made my legs turn to jelly. I grabbed at the wall for support. No help in sight. The last time I saw my co-worker, she was baled up by a group of them and I hoped she would survive. She seemed to be capable of talking her way out of anything, yet they were too overwhelming for me to even stand a chance. I could hear them coming closer, their feet pounding louder as they drew nearer. Their cries of defiance filled the air and I shook. Then they saw me. I lost all control and fled. They were immediately after me, with devilish cries that resounded with their excitement of the chase. I fled. What could I do? I ran this way and that, dodging the trees and any equipment in my way, making for whatever safety the outbuildings might give me.

They whooped with glee and pounded after me, their weapons held high in the demonstration of their power to instil terror. I dashed around the corner and ducked into the nearest door.

As I squatted cowering in the corner, I looked at my watch. Five to three. Oh God, only five minutes more and my first day of kindergarten placement will be over.

Footprints

'It's quite extraordinary how the years have all gone by,' she thought as she sat enjoying her morning cup of tea, watching the rain. She smiled at the indents in the concrete path that were filling with water and drifted into her memories.

Jaye came in all dirty and sweaty, but looking so pleased with himself. 'I've finished,' he said, wiping his brow with his sleeve. 'It looks really good. Took ages to get the whole lot smoothed.'

I smiled at him. It was always so important to him to do things well.

'Come and see,' he said, followed by his wonderful boyish grin. 'Come on, I want you to see how good it looks.'

We rounded the corner and 'Bloody hell! Just look what you've done!' Jaye shouted angrily.

Before us, we saw Billy trundling towards us over the still soft cement with a mirrored grin of his dad's and a bunch of soursobs in his chubby little fist. His face crumpled and wobbled into fear while tears welled at his daddy's angry voice.

I put my hand on Jaye's arm. 'He must have got out the back door again. We do need to fix that latch.'

Billy stood transfixed in fear and sadness with tears running down his face from his now closed eyes and wails sounding louder by the minute. He was slowly sinking.

'Oh shit!' said Jaye and then crossly, 'Billy, come here!'

Billy decided it was too much to bear to have his beloved daddy shouting crossly at him again. Howling loudly, he raced towards me as fast as he could, still tightly clutching the soursobs. He flung himself into my waiting arms and began sobbing broken-heartedly, desperately looking at his daddy after turning his head and leaving copious snot and tears all over my top.

'Oh shit,' said Jaye in a different voice.

'Oh, Jaye,' I countered, 'he didn't mean it. The path wasn't there last time and he's only two.'

Jaye nodded and struggling to control himself squatted down. 'It's all right, come to Daddy for a hug.'

Billy shook his head and buried his face into me again.

Jaye reached over and stroked Billy's hair. 'I'm sorry I shouted, matey. It's OK. You didn't do anything wrong. Daddy loves you.'

Billy raised his head and sniffled loudly.

'Come here, matey,' Jaye said coaxingly, holding out his arms. 'Come and give Daddy a big hug.'

Slowly Billy released me, stumbled over to Jaye and sank into his arms and began sobbing again.

Jaye kissed Billy's hair. 'It's OK, matey. It's OK. We can fix it.'

I said, 'No, let's leave them.'

'What?' said a startled Jaye.

'Yes,' I replied. 'Let's leave them. One day, Billy will be all grown-up and gone. Now we have a permanent memento of him.'

Jaye did that gesture of rubbing his hand repeatedly over his hair which I knew was associated with him trying to come to terms with dilemmas. He turned and looked at me.

I smiled. 'Honestly,' I said, 'we'll have a really unique path.'

He smiled back wanly and turned to look at his perfectly smoothed path, its full length now dotted with the footprints of a very small bare-footed boy. Two deeper holes stood out in the middle.

The Duel

The atmosphere is tense. The outline of the battle is drawn and my opponent and I are preparing ourselves as best we can. I feel I have experience on my side, but the suppleness of his youth is very apparent.

It's time! Without hesitation, he makes his first move. I am impressed with his clear decisiveness as I retaliate with my own strategy. We thrust and parry, each making our own mark. Is it the rattle of bones I hear, or just the clicking of the dice of fate? The tally of our scores against each other rises and my state of mind and breathing start to become challenged. He's so obviously confident. He makes each move with the grace of a winner, whereas I'm sometimes hesitating and often feeling put on my back foot. Calculations run through my mind. I can't miss an opportunity. He's quick. His turn, now mine, his, mine. I continue gamely, he with many a flourish. I must keep my wits about me; my honour is at stake. I feel the importance of this settle around my shoulders like a weighty mantle as my arm again reaches out in defence of my position. He casts me a cool smile, slightly cheeky, I feel, but I determinedly manage a grimace back. I am not one to be beaten without exercising all my talents and strength of mind.

Oh no! I can feel the end approaching. I've just missed an opportunity and fate has taken the pen and written down my error. My adversary now has a greater advantage and he strikes quickly. I lean back, but not in defeat. Not yet. No, never. I valiantly reach out and try again. But he's quicker. A lunge, a roll and it's over.

Lost, lost! I sink down, head bent in defeat and surrender. Lost! I try to take it in. I've lost. My number's up in one of life's games of chance; lost to the roll of the dice.

My grandson cheers. He's still Yahtzee champion.

No Compromise

'Shit, I hit them!'

'Bloody hell, Tim!'

'Well, it's dark and they had dark clothing and…I didn't see them.'

'Step on it, Tim. Let's get out of here.'

'But Dad, we have to stop.'

'Not bloody likely. I'm not having this get in the papers with my promotion just confirmed. Step on it and fast.'

'But Dad, they could be hurt.'

'Get going! Now! You're still on your P plates and you'd lose your licence, not to mention it's my bloody car.'

'God, what if they die? I don't even know if it was a man or a woman I hit. What if someone saw us drive away? Dad? What if someone did?'

'They won't have. It's dark. Just keep going. We need to get home and clean the car.'

'Clean the car!'

'Yes, get it looking OK, and fast.'

'Dad, all you can think of is your promotion. What about the person hurt?'

'Don't give me that. You and your sister get it pretty good because of me. So does your mother. Bloody hell, Tim, you've dented the front panel and smashed the light! You're going to pay for that out of your allowance, my lad, no matter how long it takes you. Right, now you wash the car. I have to ring Bill and see if he can fit in the car first thing in the morning.'

Bastard. All he thinks of is himself. Pay for it, yes, I'll pay for it all right. The person may be dead. Oh bugger, now I'm drenched; the hose wasn't connected properly. Oh God, it's their blood and…and hair. Oh God.

'Tim. Tim, wake up! I've booked the car in for six forty-five. You'll have to take it there. I've got an early press conference and we need to finalise my speech. Bill says he can have it finished in about two hours. That should be early enough.'

'Early enough for what?'

'In case by any chance there was someone who saw the plates. There'll be no evidence of damage, and then it couldn't have been my car. The witness will obviously have made a mistake.'

'So you do think there was a chance someone saw us then.'

'You always need to cover your back, Tim. How many times do I have to tell you? Now get going. Bill's starting that early as a special favour to me.'

'Bet he doesn't know we hit someone.'

'Of course not, stupid. I told him we hit a 'roo.'

'In St Barnabas?'

'No, clot. I told him we did it on the weekend. Right, I've got to go. Don't you worry. Everything will be fine. No one will even know after Bill's handiwork.'

'I'd like to report an accident that happened last night at about seven p.m. in St Barnabas, near Tremore Street. It was a hit and run. Yes, I know who was driving. I have the car outside. Is the person badly hurt. Are they OK?'

Repentant

'Oh my God!' Cheryl nearly sobbed as she picked up her sodden chewed manuscript. 'Why did you have to buy the wildest, most manic puppy there?'

'He was quiet when I chose him,' Jim said, defending himself and then picking up his now unrecognisable left shoe.

'Probably sedated,' muttered Cheryl, her throat constricting as she collected the broken pieces of the vase her mother had treasured.

Just then an ominous crash sounding outside sent them racing to the French doors to survey the next disaster. Timmy was vainly trying to catch the boisterous Kimbo, and another ceramic pot smashed in their wake.

'He's going to have to go back!'

'Oh, come on, Cheryl. All puppies take time to settle.'

'My ferns! You can fix all that…' and her gesture took in all the earth, broken shards and bedraggled ferns spread over the patio.

Squeals of laughter floated over to them from the puppy and the boy rolling on the lawn and they exchanged rueful grins.

'He'll be OK, you'll see. I'll get some more pots tomorrow. For now, I'll just soak the ferns,' and Jim gave one more glance at the pair on the lawn, now playing tug of war with what looked suspiciously like his favourite old gardening T-shirt, and stepped out onto the patio to clean up the aftermath.

The morning sun streamed in the open window and Cheryl stretched luxuriously, savouring the peace and quiet. Peace and quiet! With a quick glance at Jim still blissfully sleeping, she bounded out of bed and went to investigate the whereabouts of her son and his puppy.

The two adventurers were long gone. An empty box of cookies on the sink, with many crumbs on the floor, was evidence of at least some supplies taken. Then she noticed that on the bench were the remains of sandwich preparation and the fruit juice carton not put back in the fridge. The open gate at the bottom of the garden showed they'd gone off exploring.

She wasn't too worried in the morning, as the sky looked clear and, although the puppy was boisterous, a good ramble in the woods never hurt a boy and a dog. But, come late afternoon, the clouds rolled in, black and heavy with rain, followed by a faint rumble. Boy and dog would get wet if not home soon.

Oblivious to the impending storm, Timmy and Kimbo were having a great time.

'I was a bit worried when you disappeared after that rabbit but you're a fast runner, you'll get him next time,' consoled Timmy and he was rewarded by a puppy grin with fast tail wagging before the next dash off through the trees.

'Wait! Kimbo, stop! We gotta go back the other way!'

The boy was led by the dog, not understanding yet that a puppy will follow a boy anywhere if the boy walks away.

Timmy was puffed out and he'd had enough now. 'Kimbo, we gotta go back. Kimbo, come here, boy!'

The answer was a very loud boom overhead and the sudden downpour drenched Timmy as he raced for the nearby ruins of the little stone chapel.

Crouched in the corner shivering now, as the air had cooled considerably, he looked through where the wall used to be and saw the frightened puppy hurtling towards him.

'Here, boy. It's a bit drier. Don't worry, it's only thunder,' he soothed, as the shivering little dog cowered in his arms whimpering.

Both boy and puppy huddled together as the storm raged on.

The wind had risen now and Cheryl and Jim's voices were blown away.

'Timmy! Timmmyyy! What'll we do, Jim? It'll be getting dark soon and this storm's not going to let up.'

'We'll go back and get Tom and Ethan and maybe Bradley if he's home. They can help us.'

'I'll get Mick and Brian and we'll spread out. The woods aren't that big and I'm sure Timmy's found shelter somehow. He just can't hear us.'

Another clap of thunder rolled out in the distance.

'At least that seems to be moving off, but I don't think this rain will ease. It's still quite heavy.'

They both ran off to get their neighbours.

Timmy was really cold now, although Kimbo was a patch of warmth he had curled over protectively. Both shivered, one with the cold and the other because his world had suddenly changed. Pressing himself closer to the wall beneath the partial remains of the roof didn't protect Timmy completely from the wind, but somehow brought some solid comfort.

'Mum and Dad will find us,' he told Kimbo reassuringly, stroking the puppy's silky ears.

In return, Kimbo emitted a high-pitched yowling as the next crack of thunder boomed.

Timmy's 'It's OK, boy,' did little to soothe Kimbo. His confidence in the world was breaking into little pieces; his only small comfort, the arms of his young master. If puppies could talk, he would have reiterated again and again, 'I'll be good. I'll be good. Really, really I will…'

What Has He Done Now?

'What has Tommy done now?' sighed Mum, exasperation evident in her voice.

We all crowded around her at the dining room window, watching Mr Russell, the school headmaster, walking up our driveway with Tommy following at his heels, head down, kicking stones. One skittered in the direction of the welcoming cat, who fled at such a disheartening sign of recognition. At the resounding knock, Mum lifted her shoulders, inhaled audibly through her nose and went to answer the door.

Tommy tried to squirm past Mr Russell to get to his mother, but a hand reached out and grabbed him by the scruff of his neck.

'This boy,' started the agitated headmaster, 'has no sense of propriety, none whatsoever.'

We all hung breathlessly waiting for the latest prank to be revealed.

'Stones in the hubcaps again?' I offered.

'No, probably not,' whispered Sally. 'He's done that twice already.'

'Smelly garbage in a bag, left under a teacher's desk? That was a real yelling time that was. Maybe a fart cushion in the teacher's lounge… he hasn't done that since last year,' ventured Jimmy.

'Do you have a dog, Mrs Saunders?'

The query puzzled Mum; I could see her eyebrows rise and a small frown start between them as they settled.

'No…well, we didn't this morning. You haven't gone and kept a stray dog at school, have you, love?' came her hopeful response.

'No, of course not! That would be easily dealt with. I've come here because of what Thomas acquired from the dog.'

Tommy made a face and twisted, trying to get out of that ignominious grip. He hated being called Thomas.

'Pardon?' Mum's puzzlement had now extended to her voice.

'Maybe he's got fleas,' volunteered Kathy in a loud whisper that was overheard from our vantage point behind the lounge door.

'Sshh,' I hushed too late, ducking back and pushing the others as three people's heads turned in our direction.

'I am referring to the deposits that dogs leave for anybody to step in,' he went on with.

'Deposits?' said Mum weakly, looking vaguely around for support, but Dad wasn't home and we were 'indisposed', so to say.

'Yes, madam. Your son found it funny to collect such deposits and place them where some teachers, myself in particular, would unknowingly step.'

'He did?'

'Yes, in the teachers's car park, just where one steps before entering a car. Cleverly disguised by sand, I might add.'

Jim snorted with laughter and we ran.

'It's no laughing matter, Mrs Saunders,' we heard as we fleet-footed it away and 'Cowards!' from Tommy

'He's really done it this time, hasn't he?' quavered Sally when we stopped in the safety of the backyard.

'Is Dad gonna be cross this time, ya reckon, or just laugh?' Jimmy said as he held his nose and bellowed, 'Poooheee!'

'Stop it! You're just making it worse. Mr Russell easily heard that,' I said as Sally clutched at my hand with 'Do you really think Dad might punish him, Jenny?'

'He'll have to, Tommy's gone too far. Dog turds really smell. And in the car…yuk!' Kathy made a face.

Then we couldn't help ourselves and we all burst into laughter.

'Poor Mr Russell,' I said when I could.

'Wonder who else he did it to?' Jimmy added. 'Have to be Old Spencer… Tommy really got ticked off when the old coot took away his favourite yo-yo just for swinging it too close to Jilly Wilson.'

'She didn't mind,' offered Sally. 'She likes Tommy.'

'You bunch of blighters!' came bursting forth as Tommy joined us. 'Running away, laughing like that.'

'Well, it was funny…who else did you get?' Jimmy eagerly asked.

Tommy grinned. 'Mr Spencer and that toad Mrs Adler.'

'Oh Tommy…no! How could you, she's just an old grouch, that's all.' I felt for the woman; she always looked sour and miserable.

'Well, she's a stinky old grouch now, I reckon,' and Jimmy started laughing again.

'Children!' came Mum's cross voice, 'come in here, please.'

Windfall

I'm old; I feel it in my back as I climb out of my chair and toddle towards my lounge room window. I reach out and feel the luxurious texture of the velvet curtains, possibly to reassure myself that I can still appreciate things. Their rich red-wine colour also pleases my eyes. I want to see the damage last night's storm has wreaked upon my garden. It will save me the effort of going outside. The first thing I notice are all the fallen apples, bright as rubies on the green grass. The next thing I see is a boy. He's climbing over the back fence. He's either quite young, or small for his age. He struggles to get over the top and then falls to the ground rather than jump confidently. He makes a straight line to the apples.

'I'm not too young! I can too do things to help!' I know I'm muttering out loud, but it isn't fair to be always told I'm too young, or too little. And…I'm so hungry! I've come to the old lady's back fence. It looks so high but I've brought the wooden crate Mum uses to put the washing in. She won't be using it till next week – she's run out of soap. I'm so hungry, my tummy hurts. If I put it on its end, I might just be able to reach the top and pull myself up. Oh, it's not fair. Why can't I be bigger? I'll have to get a stone or something to make it higher. If…I can…just…pull my leg up… 'ooray…got it. Ow, that hurt. There's a splinter or something and it's in my knee. Up and over. Oooh…well, now I'm down. Wow, look at all those apples. I knew there'd be some.

I'm fascinated. At first he started to grab them and pile them into a bag he'd brought with him, stuffed in his shirt. Now, he's cramming some into his mouth, as if he can't wait. Surely he can't be chewing properly. It looks more like he's really hungry than just wanting to taste one. I know the times are hard. Maybe the little bloke goes without food a lot; must do, to make him need to steal. But he's only taking the windfalls from the ground. I used to do that when I couldn't reach any and was too afraid to climb the tree. Maybe he'd like some of those cookies my daughter brought over yesterday. So I gingerly make it to the back door, open it and call out, 'Boy, would you like some cookies to go with that apple?'

'Aaaaah!' The old lady. Run, quick. Oh no, I forgot how I'm going to get back over the fence. Run, quick, she's too old to catch me. 'Oooww.'

Oh dear, he's frightened of me. Maybe he thinks I'll be angry about the apples.

He's run to the back fence and the poor love hasn't even thought about how he's going to get over again. Now what's he going to do? There he goes, running past the vegie garden. Whoops, he didn't see the channel Bob dug around it for the water run-off.

'Stay there, boy. I'm not angry! Stay there. Are you hurt?'

Sob. I can't move anyway…sob…sniff. Sob…my ankle hurts…sob… real baaad…sniff.

Poor lad, he looks so scared. 'Have you hurt yourself. boy? Looks like you've twisted your ankle. Here, let me help you.'

'It hurts,' sob, sniffle, 'real bad.'

'Can you get up?'

I try… 'Oowww.' I shake my head and mumble, 'It hurts too much.'

I look around. Is there anything that might help? I can't even see the wheelbarrow that used to be propped up near the garden shed. I'm too

old even to do gardening now. 'Wait here, boy. I'll go get some help.'
Then I'm hurrying as fast as I can go.

'Course I'll have to wait, I can't walk. But she seems nice. Don't seem
to be cross about the apples neither.

I'm puffing. Long time since I hurried. I better slow down, there's
really no need; he isn't badly hurt.
    'Tom, is that you? Could you come over for a few minutes? A
young lad has twisted his ankle in my back garden. Thank you. I'll go
wait with him.'
    Ten minutes, he said. I'm hobbling again; blasted arthritis.
    'Help's coming. My neighbour Tom is coming. I just phoned him.'
    Poor lad, he's been crying, it must hurt dreadfully.
    'Twisted ankles hurt a lot, don't they? We'll get it strapped as soon
as Tom gets here and can help you into the house.'

Into her house! No! Mum said I never should go into people's houses I
don't know. I must try to get up and get away.

'Don't struggle, boy. I won't hurt you. I have a great grandson about
your age. Here's Tom.'

Another old person. She's really old. He's old too. Old, they're both
old. Maybe it will be OK.

'Hi, Mary, what have we got here? Is this your great grandson I've
heard so much about?'

Strange, I'm almost tempted to say yes. I haven't seen him for more
than six months now. They hardly visit since they moved away.
    'No, this is… What's your name, boy?'

'Jimmy.'

'Well now, Jimmy, let me help you up. Then we can get you into Mary's house and fix up that ankle. Can you stand on it?'

'Ooww!' I shake my head. It hurts so much.

'Well, I have an old pram back at my house. I just got it from a jumble sale. My young grandson and I are going to make it into a go-kart this weekend. If you think you could ride in it, I'll go get it. Shall I? If not, I'll need to carry you.'

A pram! No way! I'm not a baby. Not being carried neither. 'Maybe I can hop if you take my arm.'

'Good lad. Let's give it a go. Any cake for resuscitation purposes, Mary? Cake usually does the trick.'

'I have biscuits. They're what caused this whole trouble. I called out to offer him some. I'll go into the house and find the first aid kit and leave you two fellows to get inside.'

She did? That was why she came out and yelled at me? To give me biscuits?

'Well, come on, Jimmy, let's get you inside.'

Oh crumbs, it hurts. What will Mum say? Oh bum, I've ripped my trousers too; just look at that. Blood and all as well.

Biscuits with juice for Jimmy and tea for us rescuers; this rescuing business is hard work. First, the bandages; here they are, and plenty, that's good. I noticed his knee as well.

'There you are then. Good work. Sit down here, Jimmy. Tom will need to wrap your ankle. I'm not up to getting down on my knees any more.'

'Well, Mary, I'm a bit stiff at times too. Maybe Jimmy could sit on the table and I could use the chair.'

The table? Blimey, what would Mum say? That does feel a bit better. Gee, these bickies are good. I'm sooo hungry and only had a couple of bites from that apple.

The boy's famished. Look at him eat those biscuits!

'Mary, Jimmy obviously likes your biscuits. At this rate there won't be any left for us.'

Choke, cough. Oh no, I'm so hungry I forgot to be nice; cough.

'There now, a good slap between the shoulders always helps, I say. Don't you agree, Mary?'

Sob, blubber, cough. 'I'm sorry,' sob, 'I didn't mean to be greedy.' I am a baby, I'm crying.

'It's all right, Jimmy. You are just a bit overwrought and seem so hungry. Are you not getting enough food, lad? I think that's what's happening, isn't it? That's why you came for the apples?'

I nod glumly. Here it comes. Now, after all those yummy bickies. Now they'll whack me and tell Mum. 'Me Dad's away at the war and me Mum can't work yet 'cos of the new baby's crying a lot. Me other brothers and me sisters try, but we can't always find stuff chucked out that's good.'

'Oh, you poor lad. Tom, do you think you could fill my wheelbarrow and take all the apples that have fallen off the tree to Jimmy's mother? I can't give you the ones on the tree, Jimmy, because my grandson and his boy are coming to pick them next week.'

I'm so excited. 'They should be all right. They only blew down in the storm last night.'

Food, I can bring home some food! The others won't ever say I'm too small again.

'Of course, Mary. How far away does your mother live, Jimmy?'

'Just off Turner Lane.'

'It sounds like your mother will be pleased when we bring the apples. What will you do with your windfall?'

'Eat some. Then sell the ones left over, maybe, if there's not many bruises. Mum'll make apple pies too, 'cos then she'll have some money to buy some flour. Apple pies make the most. We done it before.' Whoops…didn't mean to say that.

'So that's where all my fallen apples go,' I say, smiling.
    He seems surprised. Didn't he think I noticed?

I'm a bit jumped. She's noticed.
    'First time I've done it. Never been such good ones before, though.'

'Mine will all be gone next week. What about yours, Tom? Any of yours still lying around?'

I smile at her. I think she's a new friend.

I smile at him. I think he's a new friend. I notice Tom wink at both of us.

Written In the Dust

The crowd had gathered like a flock of crows eyeing off a fresh carcass. The groans of the timbers, while they were torn asunder by the maw of the grasping machine, echoed mournfully through the old garden. The windows were sightless and the front door swung open as if with a silent cry. I felt the old house was in the throes of death as it crumpled down into a scattered skeleton.

To me as a boy, the house, old and dilapidated even then, had felt alive with an unseen menace. Half-blinded windows had watched as I'd walked by and tentacles of ivy reached out in the breeze. It had been in fourth grade when our gang, as we liked to call ourselves, felt our manhood needed testing. The old ghost house provided the perfect test for bravery. Of course, it had to be at night and we'd all met with secret whispers and pounding hearts at the appointed hour. Well, after our bedtime, in the darkness of the thin crescent moon.

I would always harbour a fondness and a yearning for those safe days and nights of that little seaside town. In those times, boys could ramble undisturbed and intent on adventures. Householders slept with open windows and unlocked doors. No suspicious cars roamed the streets past ten o'clock, only the local police, who made one obligatory circuit before bidding the sleeping neighbourhood goodnight.

We'd crept unseen from the bushes after the tail lights of the patrol car disappeared around the corner. Typically, Tom's torch didn't work and he'd clutched my sleeve as, crouching low, we made our way to the back of the house. All of us had lost our veneer of bravado when the night bird screeched and we'd fallen in a huddle. I remember Reggie, always the tough guy, was the first to recover, hissing at us not to be idiots and we'd ventured forth again.

The screen door hung sideways off its hinges and the other door creaked loudly as we pushed it open. Something swooped at us and despite myself I had yelped.

'Bats!' had informed Reggie's cool superiority.

Creaking steps had led us to the top floor and cobwebs lurked everywhere. Furniture still filled the rooms and ghostly shadows flitted around as our torches grappled with the dark.

'Com'n' look at this!' Reggie had called and we had all crept warily down the hall and sidled over to stand beside him, hopefully expecting something gruesome.

He stood there shining his torch and spectral images of our faces loomed in the dirty surface of the mirror. Written in the dust in large letters was the word, 'Beware'.

Recalling later, a strong wind must have arisen while we stealthily explored the old mausoleum. As we all read that ominous word, a sudden scratching and tapping had sounded at the window. Shadows flung themselves around the room while a moaning sound came down the chimney. With shouts of dread, we'd all taken to our heels, Reggie included.

My attention was brought back to the present by the crumbling thud of that very chimney falling down. I stayed until the dust settled and turned away, leaving my memories written there for all time.

More Women Than Girls

Deeply Etched Bone China

The one thing we never talk about in our house is Great Aunt Prunella's dinner set.

Of course, that didn't stop her forever going on about it. Firstly, she did so with enormous pride but, ever since that fateful day, it was a yearly tirade with her sharp tongue always adding to that small hard lump of guilt which every time formed again in my chest. Each time we'd made the trek to the countryside, driven through the main entrance with its huge wrought-iron gates, followed the long tree-lined avenue forming the driveway to her estate and exposed ourselves to her frosty welcome, I knew what I'd hear. Each time, I'd hoped she'd forgiven me.

I'd always loved going there; the peacocks, the beautiful lake with water lilies; the magnificent curved banister following the grand staircase and the wonderful old grandfather clock with its dulcet tones melodiously echoing through the foyer. And the afternoon teas; 'high teas', Great Aunt called them; simply scrumptious teas. Silver, multi-tiered towers, filled with magic little cakes, all iced in different colours. Light fluffy scones, with homemade berry jam and fresh clotted cream. Ultra-thin, delicately shaved sandwiches, served by the crusty old butler who insisted on the honour although it was 'far beneath him' according to Great Aunt Prunella.

But since that year when I was nine, I had dreaded our visits. Mother always said, 'We have to go because it's our inheritance and I'm not having us lose it.'

That catastrophic day is firmly entrenched in my memory, as clear as a re-wound movie. I'd been given the great honour of collecting the gravy boat from the china cabinet and bringing it to the dining table, which was being laid for the evening meal, a task Great Aunt Prunella always supervised. Tonight was a special occasion.

'An occasion that demands the best china,' Great Aunt had trilled. Then, to my great astonishment and delight, 'Since you love the china so, my dear, you can bring me the last piece, the piece my mother liked the best, the gravy boat. Personally, the teapot is my preference, it's so splendid,' she had said while lifting the said admired article, stroking the fluid curves and then replacing it reverently on the sideboard, with a last pat of approval.

On completion of the setting of the table, I was going to have a bath and put on my new dress. Great Aunt Prunella adamantly insisted on us dressing for dinner and, as this was 'a formal occasion', she had bought me a truly beautiful dress.

I loved seeing my parents all dressed in their finery and, almost as much, my brother squirming in a suit and bow tie. Great Aunt often wore extraordinary hats, with feathers pluming all over the place and ropes of pearls, or layers of jet beads. I knew my mother eyed those jet beads, whereas I'd always admired that dinner set. Its creamy shapes, the deep maroon band of rich colour and the lustrous gold trim. To me, they were fit for queens and kings and to use them made me feel regally spoilt.

I'd felt so proud to finally be trusted with the task and was taking great care to deliver my precious load. I remember, even to this day, that I could hardly breathe with the effort of concentration spent on its protection. No one knew who hadn't pulled the door tightly on the latch. Or, rather, no one dared say. But the dog nosed it open. That dog, who up to that day had been a constant cause of amusement to me, its continual snuffling into interesting corners in search of adventures, its large waving plume of a tail and its rambunctious way of using the whole body to express excitement at finding a quarry worth the chase. Then, it had seen the cat. I hadn't noticed.

'How could you not, child?' was Great Aunt's repeated later accusation.

I had been totally absorbed in my responsibility when the dog crashed against the back of my knees and the gravy boat had flown out of my hands into a graceful parabolic flight until it 'smashed into a thousand pieces', as Great Aunt continually put it. Amazingly, my hand had instinctively shot out in appalled reflex and I'd caught the saucer in mid-descent.

'That is no good. What's the point of a saucer without the jug? A gravy boat is a set. A set! Jug and saucer,' had been my only belated reward, as I still held it limply in my hand after my offering had been rejected. I never did find out what was done with it.

At the time of the breakage, though, I had stood in paralysed shock as a shriek emanated from the dining room.

'Don't tell me that's my gravy boat. I won't stand for it.'

The dog and cat had totally disappeared by the time an almost hysterical Great Aunt had reached my side, turning interesting colours of purple and red which were later remembered with interest and re-told with elaborate detail by my brother, who had been drawn, as small boys are, to the sound of a mighty good shrieking. If she hadn't considered herself such a lady, she forever reiterated, she would have given me a resounding slap.

I had only numbly stared at the pieces on the floor.

'Pity it missed the rug. Just two inches to the left and it wouldn't have smashed,' Jimmy had said, most unhelpfully, gazing in awe at me.

It wasn't until a bit later on, Great Aunt having stormed off muttering, chest heaving, eyes fierce while Mother comforted me and my tears finally dissolved the icy lump around my heart, that I sobbed out my story of the dog and how hard I'd tried to be careful. It was eventually collaborated by a very distressed cat found on top of the piano and a discreet dog puddle behind the potted palm. That, however, did nothing to repair the damage. Not even glue could do that. Ever since, I'd been called 'that horrible child'. Then I became 'that horrible girl' and lastly 'that horrible young woman'. Had I truly never said sorry? She always accused me of that.

'Not even a skerrick of remorse and my precious china smashed to smithereens. My grandmother's wedding china! Handed down from my mother to me!'

I had miserably endured the accusations and recriminations every year. No amount of championing from my younger brother, no matter how well intentioned, seemed to soften Great Aunt's hostility towards me. She seemed to have forgotten how close we been before the 'tragedy'.

Now, here I stand cradling the very gravy jug that could have rescued me from all those years of anguish. We are here in Devon, on our honeymoon, because I still love the place. Great Aunt Prunella is gone now. Her long-lost estranged sister's family inherited most of the estate by default.

Mother got the 'priceless collection of china, although it does have one piece missing', specifically worded so in the will. She boxed 'the hateful thing' and placed it in storage. 'If I had believed her so despicably mean,' she had said, 'I wouldn't have subjected us all to those horrid visits.'

I wondered at Mother's lack of understanding, or was it just her memory? Or maybe she'd been blinded by the prospect of a goodly sum of money, a nest egg, gravy on the meat? I had said I'd take it all when I was married.

So, here we are, on this beautiful spring morning, just popped into this delightful little shop to browse for a knick-knack. And there it was, tucked away near the lead-lighted bay window.

'Oh yes,' the saleswoman was saying, watching me stroke its smooth lines. 'Quite a rare piece, but not very valuable without the matching dinner set of course. I can let you have it for five pounds.'

'How long have you had it?' I asked.

'Fifteen years. I'm glad it has finally found a home.'

Fifteen years. I am bemused by fate. Only a few miles away had sat that very gravy boat which could have saved my day.

No, we never talk of Great Aunt Prunella's dinner set in our family, but as for my complete set, well that's another story.

Is That Coralie?

'Is that Coralie?'

'No,' I said and put down the phone with shaking hands.

Coralie! Was it a coincidence? No one should know that name here. I hadn't been known by that name for more than a year. 'Plenty of time for them to find you,' said my panic.

I raised the receiver again and my hand still shook. I dialled the emergency number. 'Can I speak to Detective Morgan, please. My code of access is Spandex.'

'Detective Morgan is out of the office. Can I get anyone else?'

'I don't remember any other name, and he said to call if it was urgent.'

'Is it urgent?'

'Yes, I think so.'

'You think so? Madam, it either is or it isn't.'

'It is a confidential matter and I can only speak to Detective Morgan. Can you get a message to him immediately please and tell him that Margaret Collins rang.'

'Margaret Collins. I thought you said Spandex.'

'Spandex is the emergency code word to give when I want to speak to Detective Morgan. He told me it would get me directly through to him whenever I needed to talk to him, especially if it was urgent.'

'But you don't know if it's urgent.'

'I'm worried that it might be. Please let him know as soon as possible.'

'I'll pass it on.'

'Thank you.'

'We got her, boss. It's definitely her. As soon as she hung up on us, she rang the police asking to speak to that detective…Morgan.'

'Go get her. She has to pay. My Jack's in gaol 'cos of her. Get a move on too. Those detective guys move fast.'

'Dunno 'bout that, boss. She never got to speak to him.'

'Good. Go get her before they get to suspect anything. I want her gone.'

It was no good; I wouldn't be able to sleep. I decided to go and have a drink at Don's club. There would be people to talk to and maybe someone either singing or playing the piano. It would take my mind off that phone call.

'Boss, she's not here. No sign of her.'

'What!'

'She's done a runner. Her car's gone. Hasn't taken much, though. A lot of clothes still here.'

'Get back here. We'll have to get Harry on it again. He found her once, he can find her again.'

'Oh, Detective Morgan, I'm so glad you called. It might be a coincidence, but someone rang my number tonight and asked for Coralie.'

'Pack your favourites, we'll be there in twenty minutes.'

I put down the phone and sighed. 'Here we go again. Will I ever be able to live a normal life?'

Forbidden

'Don't go through the green door'

I had understood this prohibition well before I could speak. At first, I had obeyed. Like most children, I wanted to please my mummy. But I grew. My older sister has always been of a quiet, mild nature but I am an adventurous spirit. 'Wilful sprite' was my grandmother's nickname for me.

So, when I was three, as I was told, my mother happened to glance out of the window to see me standing on tiptoe on top of the overturned garden bucket trying to reach the latch, with my sister pulling frantically on my skirt, until I toppled off wailing. That was when the gate was locked.

When five, I was caught with the key and a flashlight at nine p.m., way past my bedtime.

By seven, I had developed a great interest in lock picking. I had always been a precocious and prolific reader and apparently spy and burglary stories littered my room. My mother took no heed until, one morning, she was woken early by the new baby and happened to glance out of the window to see me industriously using all kinds of tools to try and pick the lock.

At eight, I was heard using the electric drill on the hinge screws.

Came nine and with my pocket money I'd bribed my best friend to try on my behalf. However, she'd heard of all my misdemeanours and subsequent punishments and pulled out at the last minute. I didn't speak to her for a whole week!

Ten? Ten brought boys. Boys who liked dares. A few tried their best, but somehow my mother was suspicious of boys near the green gate. Why I never considered a ladder to climb over the wall, I'll never know. My focus was on that green gate.

Eleven and twelve brought boys again for a different reason. It wasn't until I was sixteen I remembered the green gate, and then it was for that different reason: my first kiss.

Suddenly I was seventeen. I moved away and went to university in the city and the city became my home. I got caught up in living my life and when my parents died, I was happy to let my sister keep the old house in the sleepy village. I was content with money for a brand-new apartment. My sister and I had never really been close, so I only went back for her garden wedding and, by then, the green gate was covered with overgrown ivy. Purposely or not, I am unsure, because my sister preferred not to look at the green gate.

Now, I am ninety and remembering all this. Where did all those years go? I've come back to the old house and here I stand in front of the green gate. It's the same old gate. No ivy covers it. It has new hinges, a brand-new coat of green paint and even a brass plaque, would you believe. And what does it say? 'The Green Gate.'

'How original is that?' I sniff, speaking out loud. I suddenly realise my opportunity and stretch out my hand to open the gate.

'Granny Aunty,' says my little great grand niece, 'you mustn't go through the green gate.'

'Why not?' I challenge, irritation tingeing my voice and making it tremulous.

''Cos it's tresspissing,' she lisps.

I can't help myself and I giggle. 'Haven't you ever tried?' I then ask.

Her eyes widen. 'Oh no. Mummy is very sure I shouldn't.'

I allow myself to be led away to the dolls' garden tea party laid out under the willow tree.

But I am now determined. I wait until it is dark and all are asleep. I open the sliding doors to the patio and switch on my torch. When I reach the green gate, I'm quite out of breath, something that's been troubling me of late. In fact, my heart is hammering. How silly of me to be so flustered about a ridiculous gate. I reach out my hand and feel the wood with my palm. After all these years, finally! I don't notice I am gasping for breath; I'm just focusing on the gate, that interminable gate. Slowly I start to push it open. Suddenly the pain hits. It's excruciating. I gasp with its intensity. Everything goes black as I fall through the gate.

'Wonder what the old girl was doing there?' the young ambulance attendant said to the older one.

The little girl had tears running down her cheeks as she looked up at the old lady.

'Ol' Granny, she went through the green gate.'

'Yes, dear,' said her great grandmother, 'she always wanted to.'

Annie's Clock

The house had been in the family for generations. How many? As far back as the early 1800s. Not the house today, but the first house, which had been added on to as each eldest child inherited and wanted to stamp their mark. Today, it was a rambling two-storey mansion with a third storey of converted attics. I was the latest 'Inheritor'.

The house felt cold and lonely. It had been standing empty, waiting for this day, as my mother lay terminally ill. Now, she was gone and I'd been given the key this morning. I had no idea what I was going to do with the house. I was an only child and my father had died when I was young. My mother had kept it by taking in lodgers and keeping the guest wing for us and visiting family. I had a myriad of cousins and I fondly remembered the school holidays with much banging of doors, thumping of running feet and generally a shout from some lodger. All taken with a grain of salt, as the lodgers had generally been nice people. Most of them were 'long term', although Mother had always kept one room free for 'Overnighters', as she called them, even though some stayed for up to a month.

This was 'Annie's room'. Why it was Annie's room had dimmed with time but, as far as I could gather, Annie had been an orphaned relative taken in under duress and she had lived and died in the big house. This particular room was an add-on, almost a tower, and it was my favourite room of all in the house. It was high in the roof, an attic turret room, with sloping ceilings and reached by three narrow staircases, two of which had a large landing that could be used as a small room. Annie had lived here all of her life, using the landings as a sitting room and a breakfast and luncheon room. Apparently, according to a diary she found, she had been allowed during her adulthood to dine with the family in the evenings. But it was the top room, her bedroom, that was still called Annie's room. My cousin Barnaby had laughingly installed on the door a plaque saying 'Annie's Room', complete with a spray of roses. Somehow, to me, Annie wasn't associated with roses. I saw her with lily-of-the-valley. I had often climbed to Annie's room to dream my adolescent dreams and had spent many a day enjoying the glorious view.

So, today, where did I go? Annie's room. I smiled as I felt my feet fit into the indents worn into the stairs. Reaching the room, I roamed about, touching familiar objects. Everything was dusty and felt abandoned. I stood looking at the bare stripped bed. A four-poster, but scaled down to size to an overlarge single to fit against the high end of the room. I'd loved it when Mother let me sleep in that bed; it had made me feel like living in the grand old days of the past. The heavy drapes were still in good condition as they had all been replaced about ten years ago when some professor had been expected. A professor of antiquities, and it had amused Mother to offer him Annie's room.

I sat down on the bed and as I turned to look out the window, my eye caught the old clock on the mantelpiece. Yes, I remembered, the professor had been most excited. It was an original of some early Swiss clock maker, apparently. He'd wanted to buy it for his collection, but Mother had refused even the extraordinary amount he'd offered.

'That,' she'd said, 'was Annie's clock, and it belongs in Annie's room.'

So the story went, the clock was the only possession Annie had left of her previous life. Her father's family had been clock makers. Somehow, down through the years, it had become a family tradition that if any special treasure or important object was lost, it was 'up in Annie's room behind the clock'. Possibly this had originated long ago from a young family member teasing the lonely little Annie. But it had stuck, and down through the generations the saying had kept being repeated.

Now there was only me. I rose and walked over to the mantelpiece where it sat and stroked the smooth wood. Then a thought struck me. What was behind Annie's clock? Anything? I lifted the clock away to look. Nothing; only a shape made in the dust and the stone wall of the chimney.

'Ha,' I said to myself softly. 'What did you expect? A little pile of treasures?'

I was just about to put the clock back when another thought came: 'Behind the clock.' I turned the clock round so I could see the back, and there it was. The greatest treasure Annie could have had. My eyes misted over as I read the brass inscription.

To my dearly beloved daughter Annie. You will always be in my heart and, to remember how much I love you, all you need to do is look behind your clock.

Guilt

I stood in the hallway, looking at the gilt mirror. It had been in the family since my great, great grandmama's time. She had died not long after I was born. The story was that she had been a 'royal consort', something that was a clever way of saying 'mistress' as far as I could gather. It seemed she had brought the mirror to the family estate after her 'escapade' as my ninety-six-year-old great grandmama liked to call it. But then the facts got hazy.

It was my sixteenth birthday and there were two family traditions. One was that for four generations the women in the family had married in their sixteenth year. The other – though I think it must have just been coincidence – they all seemed to die in their ninety-sixth year. Well, I'd decided I wanted to break the traditions – the first one at least; the second one could wait. I stood looking at my reflection in the mirror and then glanced down to the small portrait in my hand. I could see myself there too. It was of my great, great grandmama, though; a striking likeness.

Mama's call drifted up the stairs. I didn't want to face the party tonight; she must have invited all the single young men in the district. I would be expected to mingle and consider a possible choice. I didn't want to face her fussing about my dress either, so I made my escape. I went to my favourite place, the attic above the west wing. It was actually the playroom for the children's nursery from my grandmama's childhood. She had a nanny back then who lived with the children in the 'west wing'. No one ever went there any more; it was in what was referred to as 'the old part of the house'. Where we now lived had been renovated by my parents when they married.

I climbed the back staircase that went up to the old nursery and then the narrow one that arrived at the attic. It was full of old things. 'Junk', Mama called it, but Great Grandmama wouldn't let her throw any away. Great Grandmama turned ninety-six this year, so maybe my mother would get her way soon.

For a while, I sat daydreaming at the window seat, looking out over the roofs at the hills in the distance. They beckoned me. Then I started to absently roam through the clutter of memorabilia. There were several large trunks and I vaguely remembered dressing up in some of the clothes in one or two of them. I thought it might be fun to do that again.

On opening the second one, I found some most beautiful old clothes and rummaged through them. In doing so, I discovered a wonderfully carved wooden box, locked and no key to be found. A determination came over me. I took it down to my room, deciding to look for a tool to open it after lunch. But after lunch, Mama captured me and I was bathed, had my hair dressed and finally stood in that dress so admired by both Grandmama and Mama. Much was made of me becoming sixteen and the family tradition. I refrained from mentioning the second tradition, although it might have taken their attention away from me – out of kindness to Great Grandmama, I suppose, who also enthused about my appearance. They all three were hoping for an engagement announcement at the evening's end.

The party passed in a blur of male faces until, beauless and ringless, I stumbled to bed.

The next day, I awoke to my mama's recriminations and, as I tried to blot out her tirade, my eyes fell on the wooden box. Pleading a headache got rid of Mama and I dressed and found the toolbox in the shed. Choosing the far corner of the rose garden under the lilac, I opened it. It was filled with very fine quality writing paper and a small book. I opened the first page to read 'The Diary of Esmerelda Fortescue' in beautiful handwritten script, that style made by using a quill or a nib pen with ink. Esmerelda was my great, great grandmother's name, but Fortescue? That wasn't any name I'd heard of before.

Half an hour later, a story had emerged. My grandmama twice removed was a thief! Also, a great liar! She had manufactured an aura of mystique and captured the attention of a royal prince. Knowing she could never expect to become a queen, she had helped him choose one and so continued in his favour well after he was king. But eventually, or maybe as a result of 'the royal brat', as she referred to the firstborn heir, she fell out of favour. In a fit of pique, she stole the gilt mirror. If she ever had any sense of guilt in regard to the theft, it didn't show in her memoirs.

I hugged the diary to my chest with glee. This revelation of the family's great treasure now being an object of shame might really help me be free of the guilt trip Mama was trying to lay upon me for not securing an engagement last night. I sprang up out of my hiding place and headed back to the house. I wanted just one more look at that gilt mirror before I announced my news.

In the Garden

She sat very still in the sunshine looking down at her hands. She'd always liked her hands: long, slender fingers and well-shaped nails. Now they looked old, gnarly and wrinkled with age spots and raised blue veins. She sniffed with displeasure. The knuckles were knobbly and the cuticles had hardened. Arthritis bothered her when the cold winters came. It was soothing to sit in the sunshine. She continued to look at her hands and the mist of years seemed to roll away and a memory came of another day long ago, when she'd sat in this very garden and looked down at her hands in admiration.

A beautiful, artistically designed, unusual ring had declared itself upon her left hand on the day before – the day when they had been married. She had looked up then and the flowered canopy had still been there, although all else was removed. A new life had been beginning in this old house that day. A new beginning in this old house still filled with her childhood dreams. Every corner of the garden held a treasured moment. Her parents had moved to a small cottage and given her the house as a wedding gift. She'd been so happy to find she could continue in this lovely old home, to bring her own children into its welcoming fold. She'd consented to modernising the kitchen and bathrooms and her new husband James was very keen to design them and make his mark on their new home.

She nodded off and woke a little later, still finding the sun warming her and the birds pleasantly singing. She smiled and looked down at her hands again. This time she saw the tiny finger -flowered hands of her babies, the chubby dimpled hands that clutched hers in their adventuring into this garden of delight. She turned her hands over to show her palms and cupped them with the memory of a child's downy head at her breast, the soft little bottom as one drowsed over her shoulder. Slowly she rose and went inside to make a cup of tea.

She knew what her hands would do tomorrow. They would pick a last bunch of flowers from this wonderful old garden and lay them on James's grave. Then, the day after that, the moving van was coming to take her to her new unit in the retirement village and she would only be a visitor to this garden next time she came. Her daughter was moving in with her eyes shining with bright hopes into her new husband's eyes. New children would frolic in the foliage, laugh under the laurels. Smiling into the teacup held in her hands, she saw her sons coming back from overseas and visiting next summer.

The Key To the Crumbless Banquet

Once upon a time, there was a young girl…

That's traditionally how fairy tales have started and I have wanted to write a fairy tale for some time. Yet this isn't a story filled with evil witches and princesses helpless under their spell. It's a story of how we create our own spells and enchantments and, although we don't need a prince on a white charger, we do need a key. So I'll start again.

Once upon a time, there was a young girl. Well, almost a young woman. She had accepted what she believed was her lot in life, for all that part of her life that she could remember. If she had some memory of a different time, she had turned away from it to quieten her longing. It was far simpler, it seemed to her, to focus all her energy on coping with the life she led. She had the most abundant hair, yet it hung matted and tangled around her shoulders, with the occasional leaf or piece of straw attached. Why didn't she take care of it? Because she had no brush or comb? Or because she'd lost the will to look? There actually was a brush, admittedly rather grubby, that had lain discarded from the big house on the pile of refuse, which was burned every three months or so. No, she 'kept to her lot in life', as they say: the girl who took care of the pigs. Shall I tell you her name? Or shall we leave her to be called 'the pig girl', which is what she heard herself called whenever people thought to mention her. I think I'll leave her as 'the pig girl' because, although she thought she knew her name, she'd come to accept she was 'the pig girl'.

I will say something about her that's worthy of admiration: she took good care of those pigs. But she doesn't love any of them any more. She learnt that the first time. Oh, how she'd loved that piglet.

She'd named him Horatio. It was at the time when they'd first told her it was her job to care for the pigs, and she was young enough to believe that by 'care' they meant 'love'. Well, Horatio went in all his succulent splendour into bacon, no matter how many tears and slaps were forthcoming to his small mistress. So, to preserve herself from pain, she never loved a pig again. Not even the cutest one.

It's so many years ago now, and she's so successfully buried the incident, that she would be puzzled if we mentioned it to her. Should we blame her for encasing her feelings in baked mud? For cremating a terracotta encasing on her heart and an unnamed emptiness? Hardening it to a stone wall? Judge that as forming an easy way out? I look at her and see her strength put towards her survival, because her days were hard and she toiled from dawn to dusk. All her effort went into coping with what she had learnt her life to be. Quiet, and accepted as shy, she preferred to sit under the large table at night and scavenge with the dogs for food dropped inadvertently rather than take a place and fight for her share amongst the other farm hands. The camaraderie in the jovial free-for-alls wasn't appreciated by her nature and she'd withdrawn the first time her bowl had been left empty by greedy hands. She only saw them now as pigs. So she sat under the table and survived on crumbs.

Are you feeling sad for her yet? Don't, because even if you do, she won't notice. She's playing her part in the life of the manor so well; she's deaf and blind to anything but her survival and she's done it for so many years that she's good at it. She's so good at it that everyone's proud of the pigs that are raised. That's the only time she listens. Although, I must add, she doesn't get any actual credit for it, it's the head factor who gets the praise and the extra coin passed down from the head steward. Does she get paid? No. Paid anything at all? No. When she was a small child, what was the point? Now she's grown, both they and she are so used to her doing it for nothing, why should anything change? But there are some things hidden.

Hidden is a small carved box under the boards in the corner of the piggery roof where she sleeps. Very, very occasionally, she takes it out. It's her only treasure and no one has ever noticed. The box is made of the most highly prized wood, carved into wonderful designs of mysterious intertwined symbols. It is very old and smooth to the touch. It has a secret combination of sliding panels which, when fingered into a specific sequence, reveal a compartment within. This box she remembers from a past so dim it's only a feeling. And she remembers the sequence. It's one of the few times she allows any spark of wonder to show.

The other times are when she takes the few minutes she can find in her day to feel the splendour of nature. This is the one gift she has that the others have lost. She sees in her surroundings the beauty that the others don't pay any attention to. Moonlight is the kiss that comes to her at night. The nightingale's song is her lullaby. Both sun and wind give her the only caresses she welcomes; a morning lark, her welcome to the day. The mighty oak gives the protection of climbed upper branches and the inquisitive squirrels, acceptance of her quiet presence. Sparks of light held in the night sky are her jewels.

So now, back to the box. What's inside after she's fingered the sequence? She handles the contents with great care. A fine gold chain with a cleverly worked strong clasp is strung through a hasp on a golden heart that opens as a locket. Within the locket are two hand-painted miniature portraits; on one side, a man and a woman and, on the other, a small girl of about three or so. All are dressed in very fine clothes and have happy expressions in both their eyes and faces.

The other piece of the mystery in the box is a key. Not an ordinary sort of key, but a splendid example of craftsmanship in filigree which turns it into a work of art. This key is made of solid gold and has marks of the maker's identity near the end that turns the tumblers. One thing that stands out about the key is the upper surface. A craftsman with his expertise has attached finely twisted silver to spell a name. It's when she looks at the name she remembers a feeling of belonging. Amelia. It's her name and now we know it. Whenever Amelia allows herself to hold this key, her heart remembers something, but she always puts the key back in with her golden heart and slides the box's lock back into place.

Now, let's leave Amelia and go back fifteen years to another place in time. A young woman and man are both bereft, the woman more so than the man, but in an attempt to lessen his pain, she stays calm despite her tears. They have lost a child. Not through the ordinary manner, but by deception, deceit and felony. The bungled plan of a greedy nursemaid has led her charge to be lost in the wood. She fell asleep, and the child wandered off. No amount of beating from her accomplice could compensate for the loss of the promised fortune that child was meant to bring. So those two had run off and left the child to the wolves and looked for their luck elsewhere.

But the wolves hadn't been hungry in that particular part of the wood that day and hadn't taken the child. The mighty oaks had sheltered her until she wandered into a Gypsy camp. The Gypsies had taken one look at her dishevelled golden hair, the velvet ribbon, the embroidered clothes, the fine leather shoes, and thought they'd made a great catch. But there was no news of a missing child, for the parents had been instructed to keep silent and, in doing so, had hoped for her safe return.

After days of waiting long past the chosen hour of delivery, stricken by their grief and assumed death of their beloved daughter, they had fled the manor and gone to live overseas. So the Gypsies, on hearing no possibility of a child to be reclaimed, sold the fine garments and clad her in some ragged clothes they had discarded but didn't keep her, because how could dark-haired, dark-eyed Gypsies explain a golden child in their midst? They left her sleeping near their abandoned campfire and she was found by the lowest kitchen boy as he collected firewood. That's how she became the 'pig girl', tongue-tied in her abandonment.

So now we travel back to the present day and the manor has come to life with a frenzy of activity. The lord and master is returning, after so many years away. His lady is quite ill. Many times she's tried to give him another child and her final unsuccessful attempt has left her very weak, both in body and mind. He no longer has the caring for his life overseas and has returned to his ancestral heritage. Although it brings memories of sadness and loss, he's found himself drawn back to his childhood home. It's not pomp and splendour nor a great cavalcade that announces their arrival, just the barking of the dogs. Travel weary, they both quietly slip into their chambers with the aid of the trusted servants they had taken with them. A quietness settles over the estate and there are whispered stories of a mystery, but no one really knows.

So how is the reunion orchestrated? Let's make it simple. This story's point is not about the reunion, it's about what happened to Amelia after the reunion. Let's make her be finally noticed by someone, probably a kind woman recognising the factor's lustful glances. Her hair is brushed, she's given presentable clothes, and now let her be taken to the manor and presented as a lowly housemaid. What about going to the extent of them giving her a name, as 'pig girl' couldn't very well apply now? They choose Mary, as it is simple and common for their time.

We could wait a year or so more and, through her diligent unobtrusive manner and good looks, have her be chosen to be elevated to the upper station of lady's maid's assistant in training; but let's not. She of course, has kept her treasured box and it's discovered during the airing of the mattresses after the particularly damp winter. Accused of stealing it, she's brought before the head housekeeper because of the girl's obvious distress and such insistence that the box is hers, so much so that she's physically fought for its possession; a completely shocking display, completely out of character from her impeccable record of exemplary behaviour. Recognising this, the head housekeeper decides the girl should be given the chance to prove her case to the mistress.

We needn't explain or describe the scene that followed, or the amazing recovery of the mistress with her fully regaining her health. What we do come to is Amelia. For now we can call her Amelia. But should we? Is she fully restored to be Amelia? Let's find out.

Of course, stunned was the first emotion applying to both Mary and the head housekeeper when the mistress fell to her knees weeping and embraced Mary, calling her Amelia.

Wait a minute! There's a major flaw in this story. How does the box escape the avaricious nursemaid and the greedy Gypsies, you are saying. You are, aren't you? Well, I am. You do remember the 'pig girl' did have some memories, even though they were deeply buried. So, one time, when she was about eight, she crept into the garden of the manor at night, her main time of freedom and, no, she wasn't afraid of the dark, it was her friend. She was sitting by the lily pond when a strange memory floated up. She walked over to a corner of the garden where 'Amelia' had hidden the box. It was a place only known to her. Her secret treasures were there. Her doll and her favourite picture book, both now rotted into the soil over the years that had passed, so the 'pig girl' didn't find them. But, the box, being of the hardest and most prized wood of all, was still intact, taken there the very day before the abduction, without her mother's consent of course. Why the 'pig girl', so usually devoid of any notion she could possess anything, would dare to take the box, we can only put down to a very strong feeling that it was hers to keep. Of course, she never went into the garden again.

Now, having placated your peevishness regarding the possession of the box, we can return to Amelia. Stunned she was. She stood there, with her crying mistress on her knees, clutching her tightly, asking, 'How? How?' Then, a stammering confession of knowing that night in the garden how to find the box, then her mistress laughing and kissing her; the master running in, expecting to find his wife's mind to be turned, but finding the box, a girl and his heart again. So a new life perchance? And the key? A specially made ceremonial key, for Amelia's coming of age. The key to the banquet hall leading to the ballroom and the grand hall, where reparation was made for the iniquities put upon her, caused by the meddlesome and tiresome infractions due to the inequality of peasant life and, beyond that, to the family vault and her inheritance.

But let's go past those confusing first discoveries, to the day of the grand banquet, the day that all the neighbouring gentry were invited to celebrate the return of a beloved daughter. Let's be with Amelia as she goes to the banquet hall before anyone else, tries the key and places herself in the position she feels she deserves. The key fits the lock. The tumblers fall aside. The lock clicks. The door's mechanism turns and she can open the door. The table is set out, all beautifully displayed and the seating allocations not yet chosen.

Where does Amelia choose? She sits under the table, in her old place and she waits for the others to come in and have their feast. She is waiting for the crumbs of their left-overs. Of course, this is impossible because of social etiquette, her being found eventually by her ecstatically happy parents and, not to say the least, her immensely beautiful and expensive new gown getting crushed and covered in dog's slobber. But that's where she places herself in her mind. Scrabbling for crumbs before the dogs can get them; trapped in her old world of deprivation and her acceptance of a meagre portion of life.

What does she need to do? Here the fairy story helps her. She needs to take her golden heart, open it, acknowledge who she really is and find in her heart the acceptance of her true identity. Then she needs to put herself in her rightful place, a reserved seat at the Crumbless Banquet of Life. Not bad for an ending if she can manage it. She doesn't even need a charming prince.

Magic Lanterns

First a sentence.

Magic lanterns, that's what she called them, and they made an illusion of beauty in that orchard one evening long ago, a substitute which I will never regret and completely changing the disappointment into delight.

Now the story.

'Tell me a story, Grandma,' she said, 'another one about when you were a little girl like me.'

I leaned back and cast around in my mind for something to tell, something that would bring to life myself as a little girl, so like the small one tugging at my sleeve, jiggling with impatience and urgent expectation.

'Well,' I said, 'I can tell you about one evening, one special evening when my mother filled the orchard with magic lanterns.'

'Magic lanterns!' she squealed. 'How magic, Grandma?'

'Well, that's what she called them, my mother. Magic, I guess, because of how pretty they were and how she hoped they might be able to change disappointment. We made them, you see. We cut and pasted and she hung them in the trees. Each with a little candle that could shine through the shapes we'd cut in the sides; stars and hearts and diamonds and circles of many sizes.

She did it because we missed the fireworks. I remember we were so excited. There was going to be a huge bonfire and all the families from our school were going to come. There was going to be a wonderful picnic with potatoes roasted in the hot coals, and the fireworks after.

My brothers and I could hardly wait. We were ready hours before, with all our chores done. 'First time in ages,' Mother had said.

Then my father came and called us to him and said, 'Children, I know how much you've looked forward to the fireworks tonight, but I regret to tell you that the car battery is completely flat. I've tried to ring the neighbours, but they must have already left.'

My little brother cried. Oh, how he cried. I bit my lip so I wouldn't, but I felt the tears in my eyes. My older brothers punched each other and ran off shouting threats for fighting.

My mother knew we needed to do something special. So we made magic lanterns. 'We can create the illusion of beauty anywhere,' she said. 'All you need is imagination.'

So we made them and she strung them up, all through the orchard, and Father collected wood and we had our own bonfire and my older brothers threw sticks into the fire making sparks fly up and the fire roar brighter. We roasted our own potatoes in the hot coals and smothered them with butter and they were delicious. I remember it was a very dark night, with almost no moon or stars, so the lanterns shone all the brighter.'

'Can we make some, Grandma? Can we make some magic lanterns?'

'Well, dear, we can try. We can hang them from the clothes line. They will look almost as pretty, I think.'

'Can we have a bonfire, Grandma? Can I throw sticks into the fire?'

'Well, dear, what if we cook them in the barbecue coals? I've got plenty of margarine and I'll get some sparklers from the shop.'

'Sparklers! What are sparklers, Grandma?'

'Well, dear, they're magic fiery sticks that you don't need to throw into a fire.'

'Do we have an orchard, Grandma?'

'No, dear, but I do have apples and we can roast them too and smother them with honey.'

'Yum, Grandma. Where are your brothers?'

'Well, dear, I think they might be thinking of fireworks tonight. But magic lanterns will do for us.'

The Money Tree

The Money Tree was a tree that was talked about in my family as a child. It was mentioned that it was fertilised with bull dung. Of course I had to grow up a bit to realise the joke. Dad often referred to the Money Tree when we were out of money again and needed something. He always seemed to have mislaid where he kept it. Of course I had to grow up a bit more again to stop offering to look for it with him.

That Money Tree, how it could have fixed all our money worries. How it could have bought me clothes that fitted rather than my cousin's that were always too big and Mum not very good at sewing. The Money Tree; I used to picture its leaves made of notes and its flowers of coins. If we planted pennies, they would grow brown; if sixpences, silver. But it was only watered with imagination and futility.

So are the beliefs of children shattered by the felling of such trees. If I listen carefully, I can still hear the falling of the gold coins as it toppled to the ground and the ripping of the leaves as it tore through the veil of the land of plenty. In my land of daydreams, carpets flew, trees bore golden fruit, unicorns came in the moonlight and fairies used my tooth ivory for knife handles. The withering of the Money Tree did something to them as well. The 'night mares' no longer could be fed hay and kept away and 'duck under the table' for dinner wasn't funny any more when hunger quacked. Still, Money Trees are toppled and fantasies go on to be self-made. I can say that I still held some games of pretend, but the difference was that I knew they were; I grew up.

At Christmas time I look at the chocolate gold-foil-wrapped coins and sometimes see them as picked from a money tree. Now, I could make my own Money Tree. Make it out of money and wire and papier-mâché or draw and paint it, or make it a woven or sewn hanging, or out of jewels and mirrors. But it will never seem to have the great possibility that early Money Tree had, nurtured by the innocence of a child.

66

Left

'Return to sender. Address unknown' was written on the envelope.

I stared at it. I had naively believed he would still be there. I had left it too long. A pang of sadness nipped at my heart and I sat down heavily in the chair. I held the letter and looked at it for a long time, foolishly willing it to be untrue.

What had the arguments been about again? The current boy? My choice of work? My future dreams? Any one of them had brought forth his grievances against me. I'd gone ahead anyway, done what I'd wanted. Left to be free of his recriminations and found myself on the other side of the world.

His words floated back to me… 'You'll be sorry…' Well, here I am back and, yes, I am. Not sorry I went away – I needed to do that to feel young and free and adventurous. Not sorry I followed my dreams – my successes may have even reached him in his small lounge room on his old TV. Not sorry about the boy I followed, who turned out to be one who cherished me and gave me two sons and a daughter. But sorry that I didn't keep in touch. Sorry that I didn't persist past his grumpiness and refusal to come and see me, all expenses paid. I should have seen his hurt and his pride as something I could have healed by a visit. But the years slipped by.

I called a taxi. I would go to the address and ask around. Maybe an old neighbour might be there; maybe someone who might know where he went.

The taxi pulled into the once-familiar street and all recognition faded away. New shops had replaced the old fish 'n' chips place and adjoining café, a new supermarket instead of the greengrocer and butcher and news-stand. I peered at the numbers on the buildings as the taxi crawled along. It came to stop opposite where the line of terrace houses should be.

A vacant lot stared blankly back at me; not only 'not at this address', but no address at all. No neighbours to ask. No one lived here any more. Everyone had left.

A Momentary Lapse of Reason

The choice lay before me and I knew that all conventional common sense and logic was telling me to withdraw.

But it was what would later be labelled as a 'momentary lapse of reason' by my family, some friends, most acquaintances and even some strangers that gave me the springboard to my new life.

To stay with my well established, profitable and enormously enjoyable career, my beautifully renovated estate, my circle of friends, both close and those pocketed for certain activities, was admittedly a strong pulling force. Yet to go with wild abandon, with exhilaration flowing through me, was like a breath of fresh air to a caged mouse, for that's what I'd felt like I'd become. A mouse or a hamster who knew the maze, who could get the rewards and had the little wheel to console them into thinking they were running with freedom. But a rat – a rat would go through the maze, find the reward, even rise to the challenge of a suddenly different maze with a newly hidden reward and then look for a way out. Climb the walls, chew at the blind alleys. Scratch to try for a tunnel.

Was I a rat? A rat to climb out, to run out on everyone who felt me so secure and comfortable. Was that deception? Had I hidden that impulse inside, together with what I truly wanted for so long that even I had come to believe I was satisfied?

I sat twirling my glass of very expensive wine as I awaited either my strongest ally or my most vehement opposition to the possibility that lay before me. But irrespective of what advice, my heart had spoken.

Everyone says that to make your own choice is the most powerful thing that can bring you to both your destiny and your fulfilment and

I agree. It had been just that, by choosing, that I'd brought myself so much worldly success. Now, another choice loomed and I was fully aware of what the consequences would be of making a choice which was totally and wholly just for me.

I looked around at all the glamorous guests in that exclusive restaurant. They oozed that confidence of only the very rich and famous. They didn't flick a glance of interest at me; I was so well known, so well placed among them. It would only be my leaving that would disturb them. Yet even that would only come as a flutter of discontent and gossip for a few days, a glitch in their self-possessed calm and status quo. Someone just doesn't take their shoes off and walk in the sand unless they are modelling for a fee, and a large fee at that. And, even then, a total pedicure would immediately be in order.

But, as I sat there, I could still see that low-hanging moon, feel the wind on my face and my loosened hair as we sailed the harbour. And he was waiting. Not for long, but patiently. Waiting for me to let my heart leap free and leave all this behind; to start a totally new life of love, going out into the complete unknown.

Five minutes until the appointed time. The time for what? My inexplicable explanation? My justification for what I knew to be my greatest opportunity? To have it fall on uncomprehending ears and cause me to risk the boat leaving without me…never.

So I called over the maître d', who came willingly to my well known face, and gave him my briefcase full of all the signed necessary papers and left him in charge of declaring to my tardy lawyer brother that I had gone. I was not going to wait a moment longer.